DC™

SUPER-PETS!

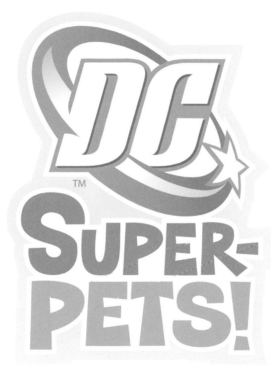

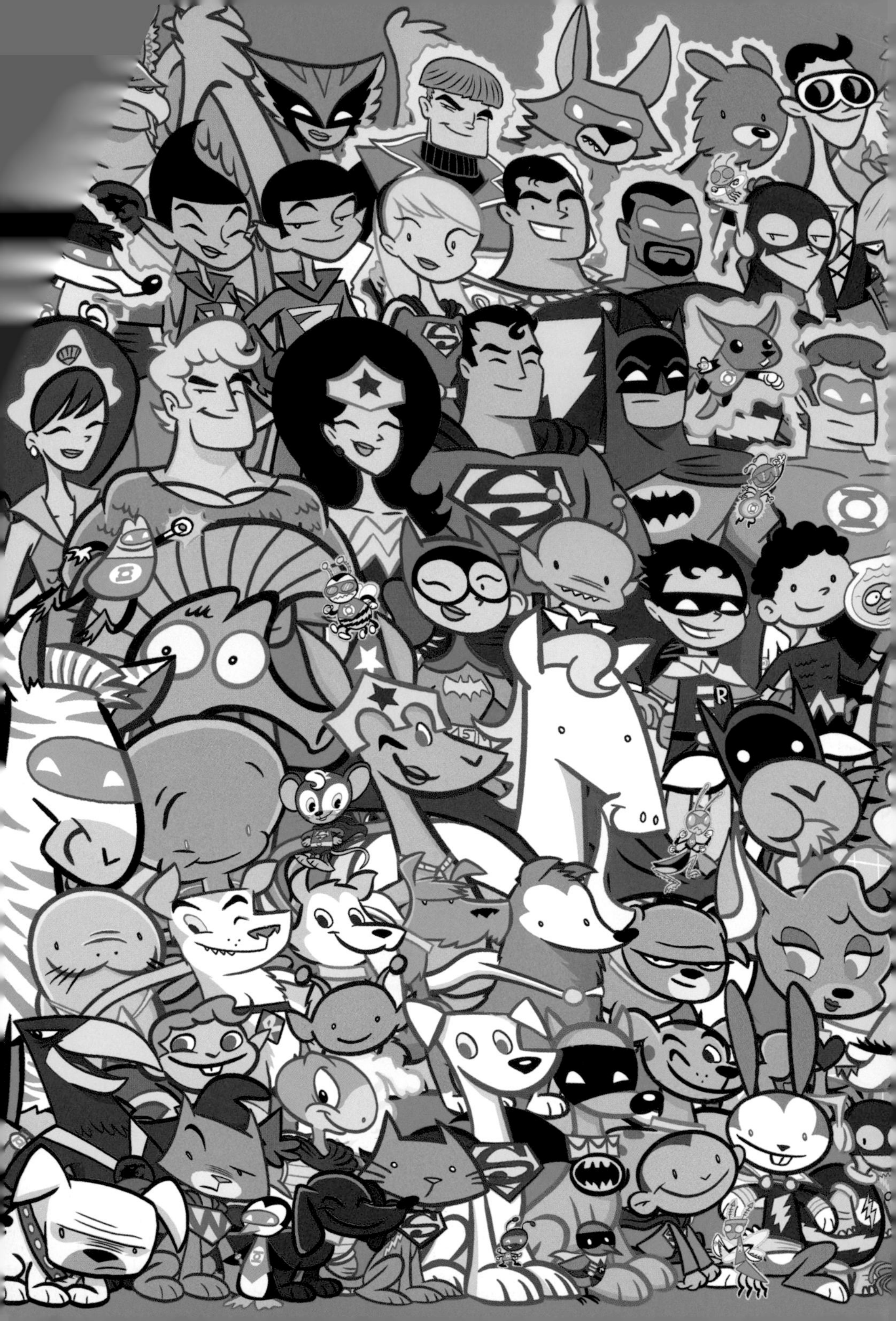

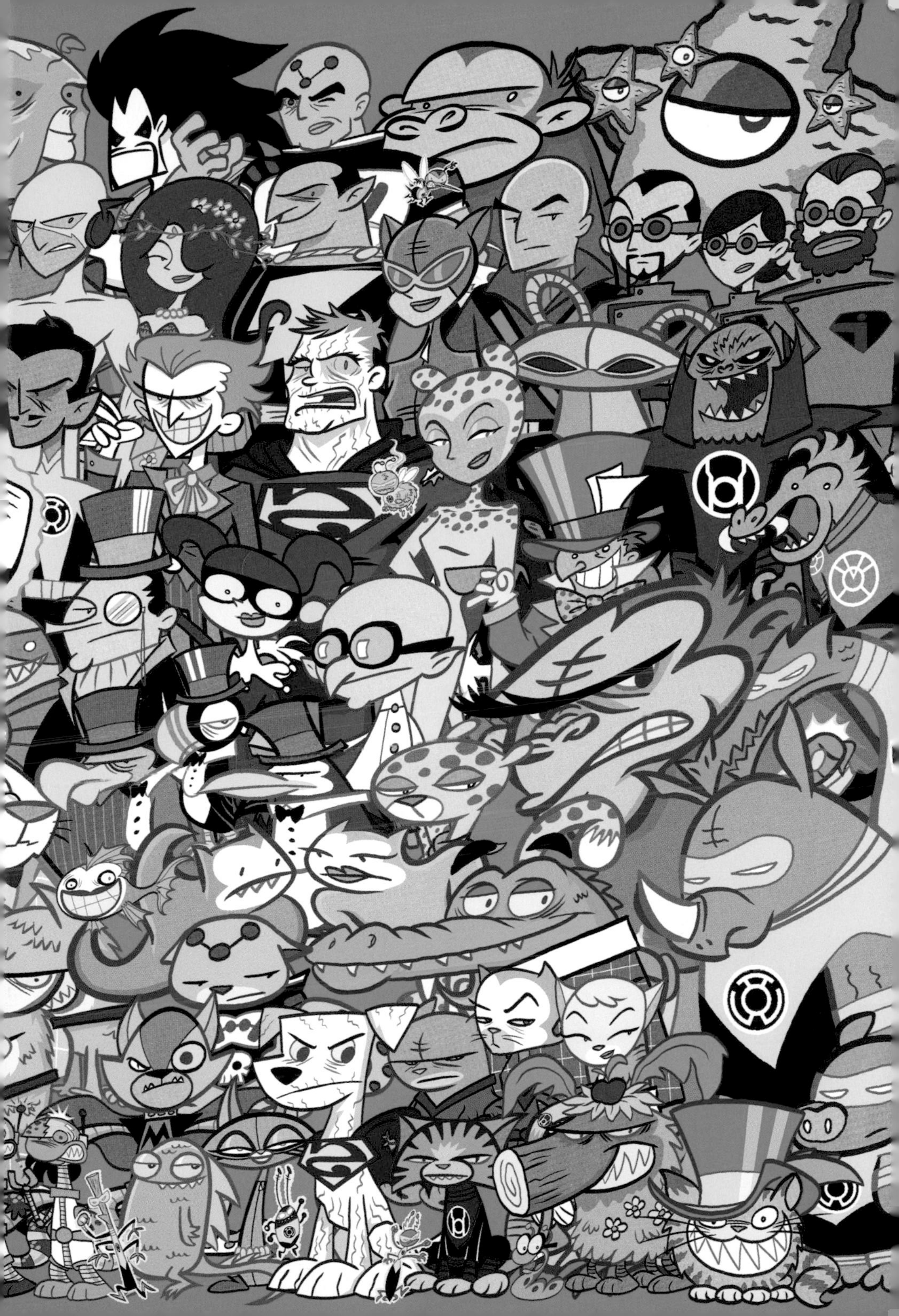

DC™
SUPER-PETS!

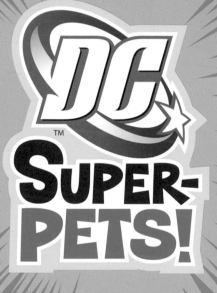

by John
Sazaklis

BARNYARD BRAINWASH

illustrated by
Art Baltazar

Batman created by Bob Kane

PICTURE WINDOW BOOKS™
a capstone imprint

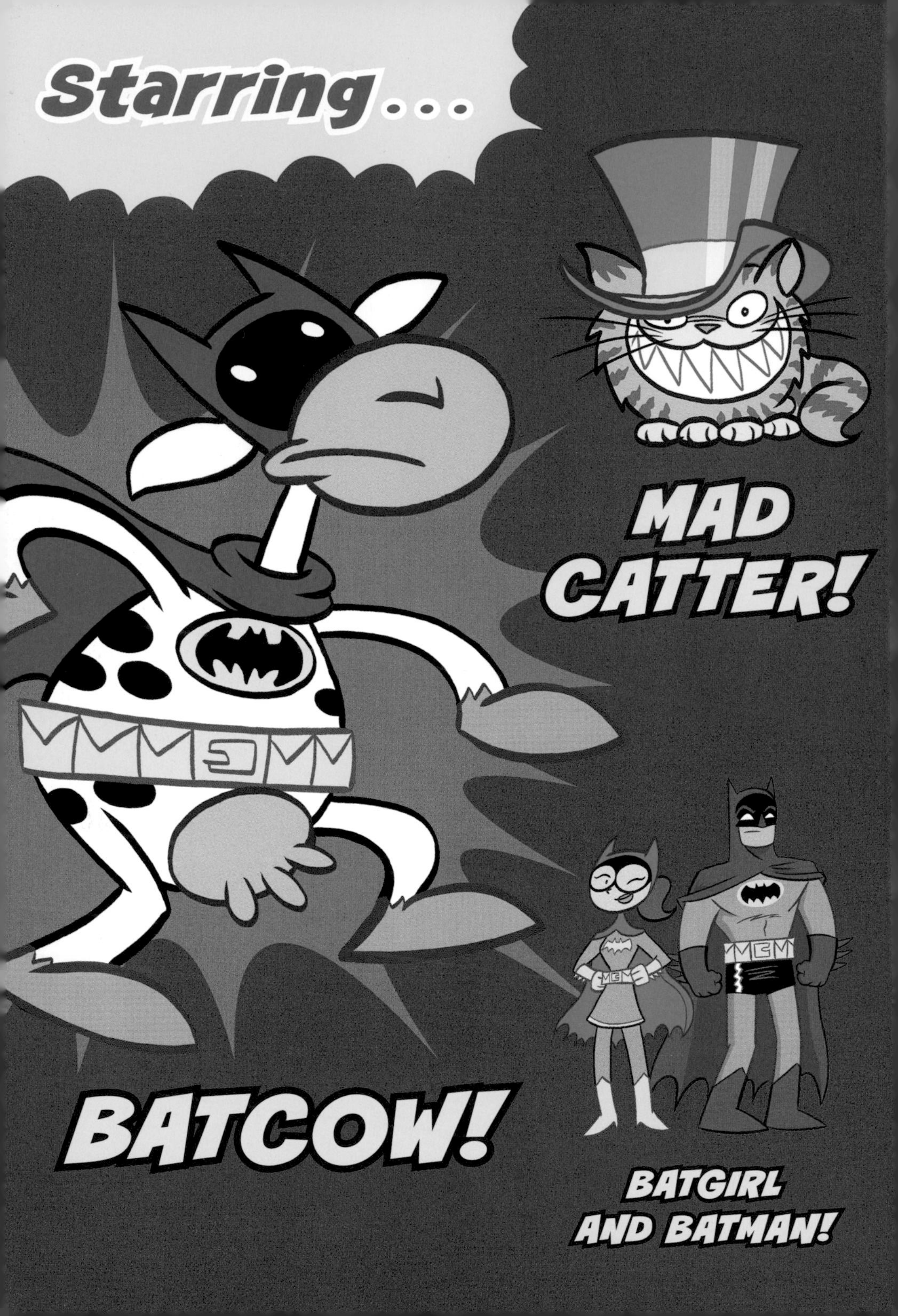
Starring...
MAD CATTER!
BATCOW!
BATGIRL AND BATMAN!

TABLE OF CONTENTS!

SUPER-PET HERO FILE 013:
BATCOW

Fireproof Cape

Cowl

Bat-symbol

Utility Belt

Super Hero Owner:
BATGIRL

Species: Holstein cow
Place of Birth: Gotham
Age: Unknown
Favorite Food: Fresh grass

Bio: To combat the udder madness in Gotham City, Batgirl taught her cow a few crime-fighting *mooves* and named her Batcow!

Super-Pet Enemy File 013:
MAD CATTER

Hypnotizing Hat

Mind Control

Evil Grin

Super-villain Owner: **MAD HATTER**

Chapter 1

FARM FRENZY

Far beyond the hustle and bustle of Gotham City is quiet farmland.

One morning, Joe MacDonald woke up early to feed his chickens. When he got to the coop, the farmer rubbed his eyes. Was he still dreaming?

The roosters and hens were wearing colorful party hats! They were walking single file. They had ears of stolen corn under their wings.

Farmer Joe scratched his head.

Farther up the path, all his pigs wore party hats as well. They, too, walked single file. They seemed to be hypnotized. Each of their curly tails looped around a pumpkin, dragging it through the dirt behind them.

Finally, the parade of animals stopped at a horse-drawn wagon inside a barn. The animals loaded the food onto the cart. Then the two horses, both wearing feathered caps, galloped out and onto the road!

Farmer Joe recovered from his shock and gave chase. He ran until his legs couldn't carry him anymore. The wagon and his crops disappeared in a cloud of dust. The farmer hung his head and began the long walk home.

By nightfall, several other farms had experienced similar capers. The police were called to investigate.

A reporter arrived to cover the story for the evening news. Each farmer gave her an eyewitness account of the mysterious events.

In a nearby tree, a fat cat sat on
a branch. He was hidden in the
shadows. He wore a top hat and a bow
tie. **The cat smiled wickedly.** In the
darkness, his evil white grin shined like
the moon.

Meanwhile, back in Gotham City, **Batman and Batgirl** watched the reports from their secret headquarters, **the Batcave.** They were the World's Greatest Detectives. However, the heroes had many partners to help in their mission, including the **Batcow!**

"It's a farm frenzy!" said the Batcow, watching with the Caped Crusaders.

"The farmers say that the animals were under a spell," Batgirl said as she paced the room. "That sounds like the handiwork of the **Mad Hatter!"**

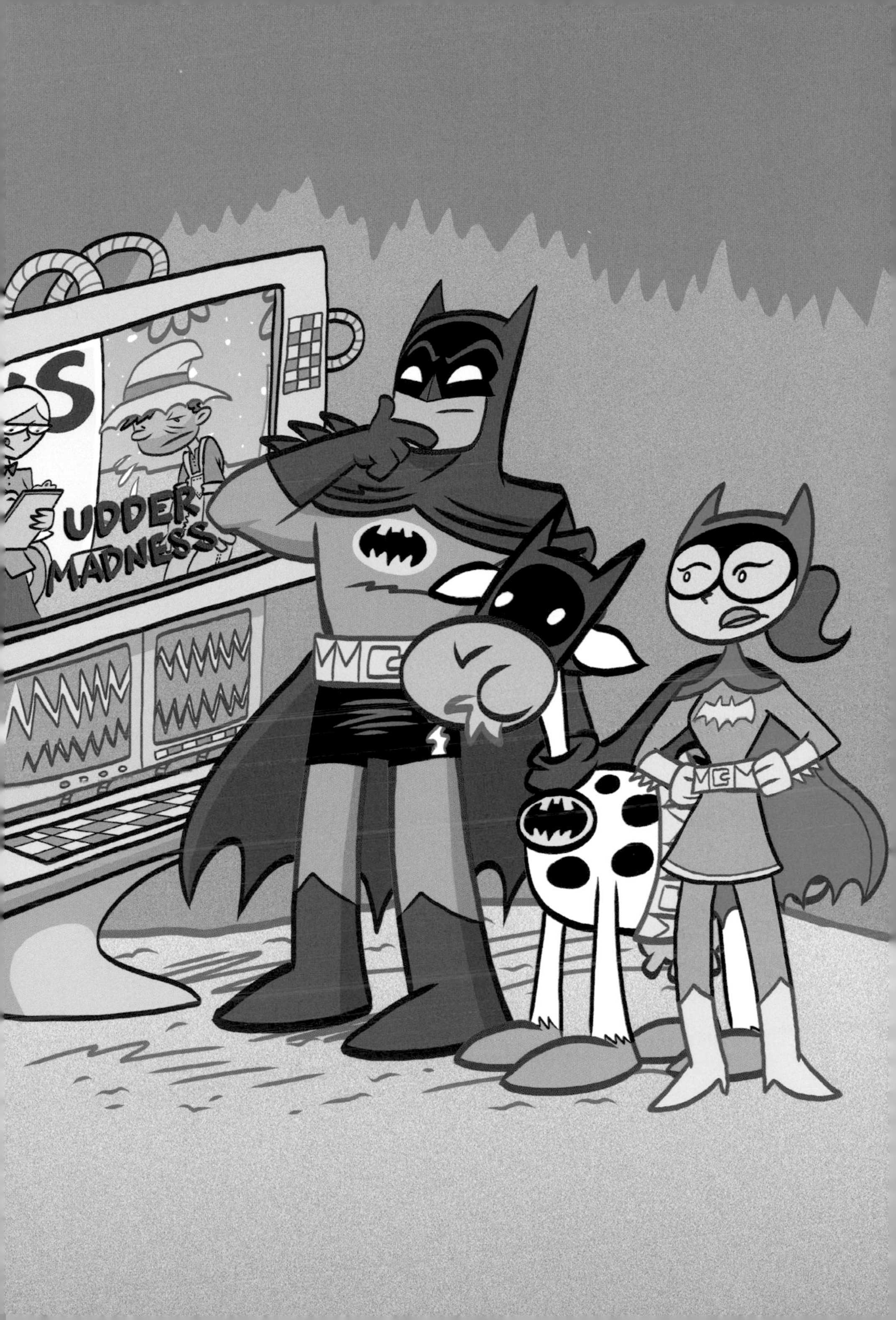
UDDER
MADNESS

The **Mad Hatter** was an evil scientist named Jervis Tetch. He created mind-control devices and hid them inside his creative collection of hats. Whoever wore the crazy caps became part of the Mad Hatter's wicked plans.

"I'll call Commissioner Gordon and make sure that Hatter is still locked up in prison," said Batgirl.

The super heroes climbed into
the Batmobile. "Let's drive out there
and see for ourselves," Batman said.
"These criminals can be crafty!"

Then the **Batmobile** zoomed out of
the Batcave.

VROOM!

Batcow turned back to the reports
on the Batcomputer. Something caught
her eye. Behind the reporter gleamed a
bright half-moon, glowing from within
the tree branches.

Batcow tapped the keyboard with her hooves. She paused the news video and zoomed in on the mystery image.

"Just as I thought," said Batcow as the shape came into focus. "The Hatter may be locked up. But his pet, the **Mad Catter**, is the real cause of this chaos!"

On the computer, Batcow searched for the nearest neighbor of the MacDonald Farm. "Merkel Meadows!" she exclaimed, finding her answer online. **"That has to be where the Mad Catter will strike next!"**

The brave bovine hopped on the **Batcycle** and headed into the night. She would put an end to the barnyard brainwashing!

ZOOOMM!

Chapter 2

UDDER MADNESS!

Arriving at Merkel Meadows, Batcow hid the Batcycle behind a large bush. Then she snuck over to a big red barn. Peeking through the window, she saw the farm animals talking excitedly.

A goat walked up behind Batcow.

"Are you dressed for the party?" the goat asked, tugging at Batcow's cape.

"What party?" Batcow replied.

"There's a mad tea party in downtown Gotham City," the goat said. "We all got invitations this morning. The plan is to sneak out when the farmers go to sleep!"

Suddenly, the animals exited the barn. They stood around Batcow and the little goat. "The Merkels are asleep," clucked a chicken. "Let's go!"

Batcow followed the animals onto the wagon. The little goat's dad was in the driver's seat. They sped off toward the bright lights of Gotham City.

Soon, the farm animals arrived at a rundown factory. They were greeted by two masked cats. One wore a flamingo mask, and the other was disguised as a walrus. But Batcow recognized them instantly as Mad Catter's **Crazy Kittens.**

The Super-Pet broke away from the rest of the animals. She hid behind the wall of a nearby alley.

The others were led to a large dining area inside the old factory. There was a table laid out with the stolen food from the farms. The Crazy Kittens invited the animals to dig in. The pigs raced to the head of the line. OINK! OINK!

At the end of the table was a TV screen. Once all the guests were seated, the Mad Catter's face appeared.

"Welcome, my barnyard buddies," the Catter said. "Please, put on your party hats and have fun. **Remember, we're all mad here!"**

The Mad Catter flipped his control switch. A loud humming startled the animals. **VRRRM!** Instantly, the animals' eyes glazed over and spun like pinwheels. The Catter's mind control was now in effect.

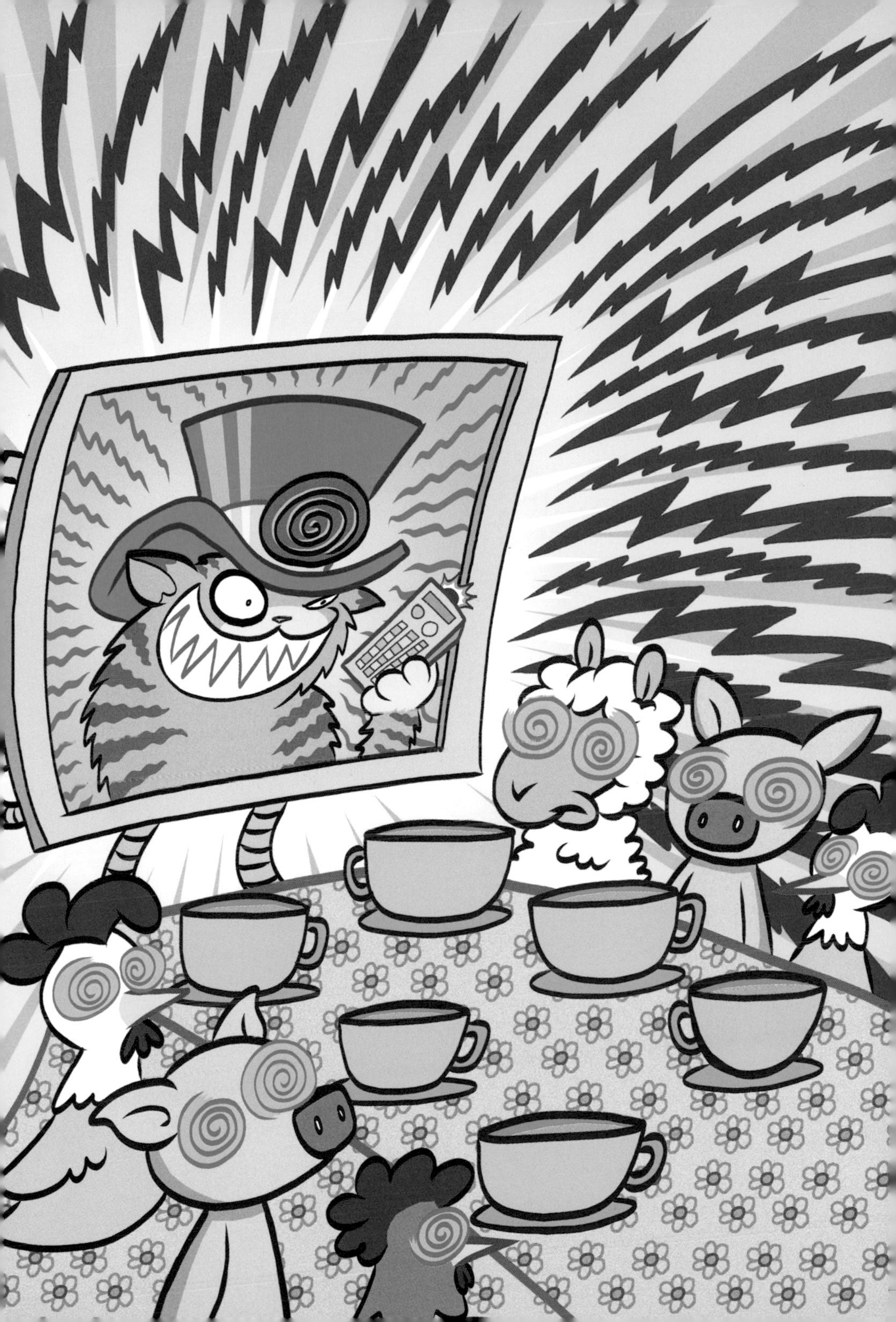

"You are now my harvest helpers," explained the villain. "Go back to your farms. Bring all the crops to me. **This fat cat is hungry for more!!"**

Batcow watched the scene through a window. "Those animals are puppets in Catter's evil plan," she said. **"I have to help them!"** The Super-Pet turned and bumped into a white ball of fur.

"You're late! You're late!" yelled a white kitten in a rabbit mask. He pointed at his watch and pushed Batcow toward the factory door.

"No, *your* time is up," said the

Super-Pet. She grabbed the kitty by the

watch chain and lifted him into the air.

"Take me to the Mad Catter,"

shouted Batcow. **"And *mooove* it!"**

The Mad Catter sat in his control room. He watched his new followers leave in their wagon. Soon, they would return with a bunch of tasty treats. The feline felon licked his wicked whiskers.

"This is my most delicious scheme yet!" the cat cackled.

Batcow burst through the control room door. She was holding the trembling white kitten.

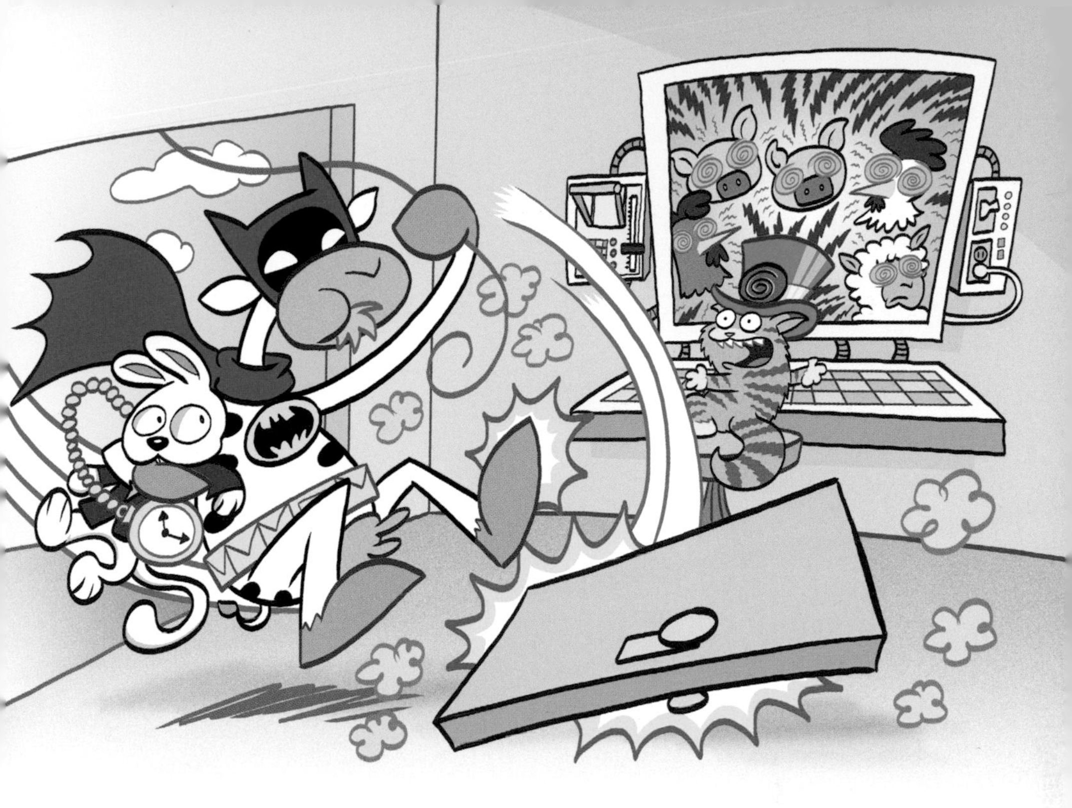

"You didn't invite me to the party," announced the hero. "So I crashed it!"

"If it isn't the Masked Moo-Cow!" hissed the Catter. "Your invite must have gotten lost in the mail. I've been dying to introduce you to my friends."

The evil cat clapped his paws together. A masked kitten darted out from each corner of the room. There was a mad hare, a dormouse, and the walrus and flamingo.

"Crazy Kittens!" shouted the Mad Catter. **"Make our guest feel** *purrfectly un-welcome!"*

Batcow glanced at her hoof. The white cat was still dangling from the watch chain. "Let go!" Batcow shouted at him. The crazy kitty plopped to the ground with fright.

Then Batcow swung the giant watch over her head. Round and round she twirled the watch and then let it loose. The watch flew straight into the Crazy Kittens, knocking them down like bowling pins. **KA-POW!**

"Get up!" the Mad Catter howled.

The kitten in the walrus mask stood first. With his sharp tusks, he charged toward Batcow. Just as the kitten tried to take a bite out of Batcow, the hero slid under a nearby table.

WHUMP!

The tusks pierced the tabletop, and the kitten's mask was stuck!

Batcow leaped for the Mad Catter, but she was tackled by the hare and the flamingo.

The dormouse kitten climbed up the super hero's back and pulled on her ears. Batcow struggled with the Crazy Kittens as the Mad Catter made his escape out a side door.

Reaching into
her Utility Belt,
Batcow pulled
out a smoke bomb.
She let it fly.

FSSST!

A cloud of gas filled the room. The

Crazy Kittens removed their masks.

They rubbed their eyes. They started

coughing wildly.

Batcow pulled out her Batrope and

quickly tied up the kitty crew.

When the smoke cleared, the villains looked all around. The Super-Pet was nowhere to be found!

"Hey, where's the cow?" asked one of the Crazy Kitties.

Chapter 3

BRAVE BOVINE

Batcow had slipped through the same side door as the Mad Catter. The entrance led to a long, empty hallway.

The villain's voice boomed through a speaker. "Give up, Bats! I've booby-trapped this entire building," he said. "Soon, you'll be as flat as a cow pie!"

Batcow heard metal gears start to

grind. WHHIRRRRRR

Suddenly, the hallway's walls started

closing in. They inched closer and

closer together. The hoofed hero had to

think fast or be flattened. She had just

the tool for the job — a laser torch!

Batcow grabbed the gadget from her Utility Belt. She aimed the laser toward the wall and fired. A red-hot beam seared through the metal. **ZZZZT!**

Batcow carved a hole big enough to fit through and pushed with her hooves. The cut-out piece fell to the ground. The swift Super-Pet leaped through the opening just as the walls pressed against each other.

Breathing a sigh of relief, Batcow took in her surroundings. All around her stood rows of glass.

She was in the hall of mirrors. In each mirror was a grinning reflection of the Mad Catter.

"Twinkle, twinkle, little Batcow," sang the Catter. **"How you wonder where I am now!"**

Batcow remained quiet.

The terrible tabby laughed. "What's the matter? Cat got your tongue?"

Batcow ignored the Mad Catter. The Super-Pet focused on each reflection — only one was the real rascal!

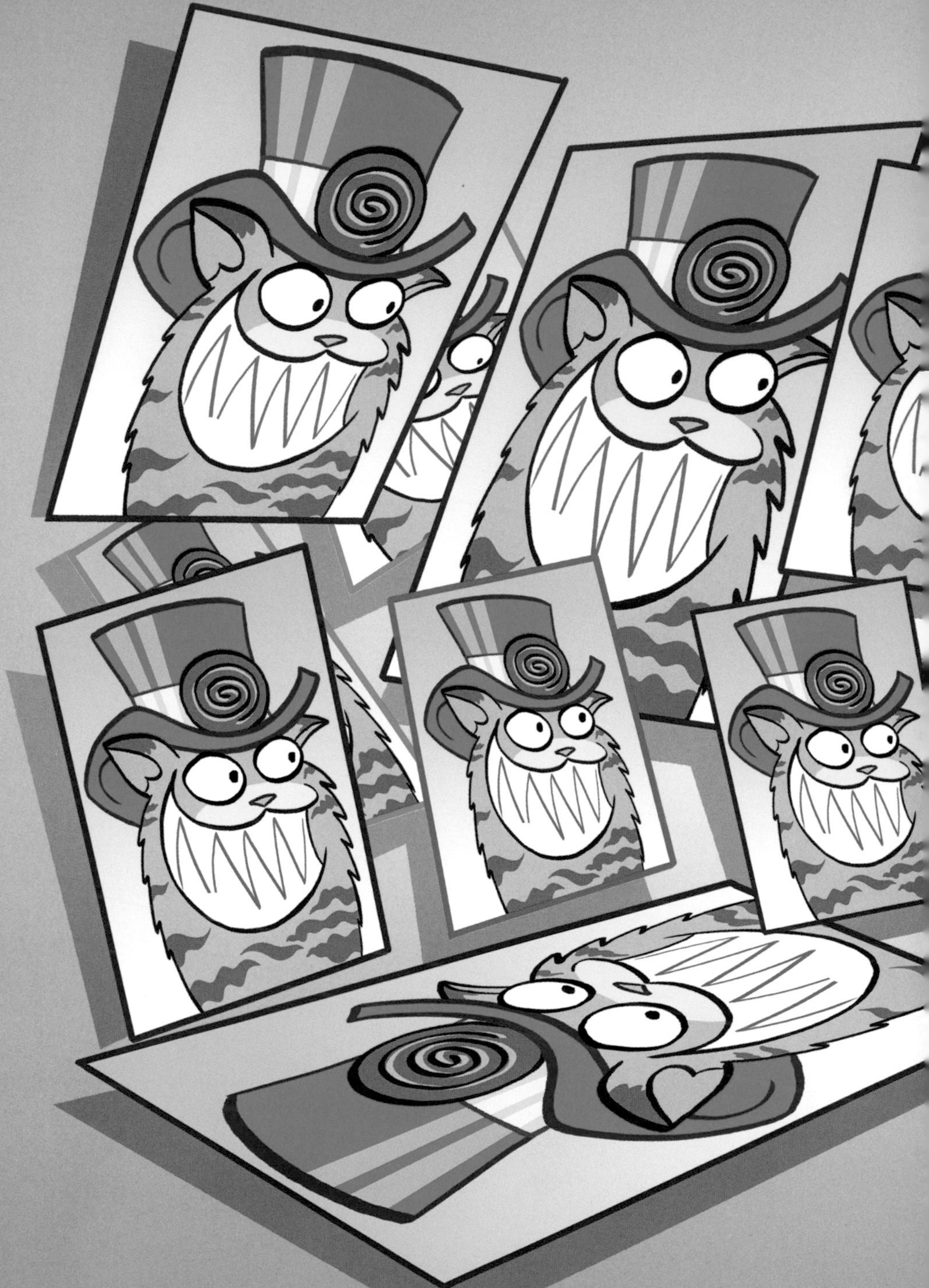

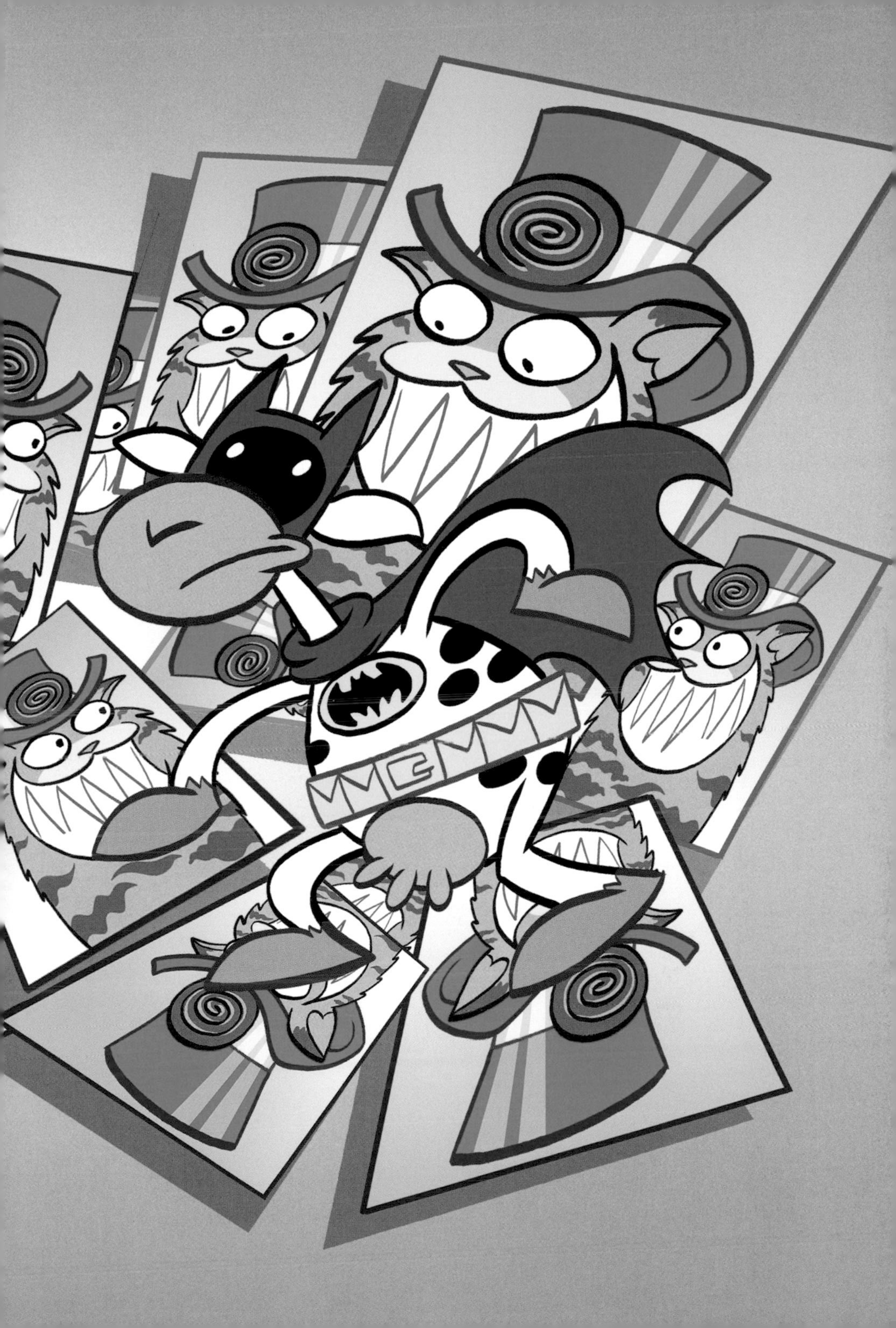

"I've bamboozled the Batcow!" shouted the cat. "After my fearsome fun house finishes you, I'll add your cowl to my hat collection. It will be my most prized possession!"

"We'll see about that," said Batcow.

The hero had another idea. She slipped on some X-ray goggles. The regular world was replaced with X-ray images. The hero could see through all of the mirrors. Moving her head back and forth, she finally spotted a tiny feline skeleton.

The real Catter had been found!

"You want my cowl?" Batcow yelled.
"It's all yours!"

Batcow bowed her head and
barreled toward the Catter. She head-
butted the mirror, shattering it.

The villain pulled down his top hat to protect him from the falling shards. Then he turned to run away.

Batcow chomped down on the Mad Catter's tail.

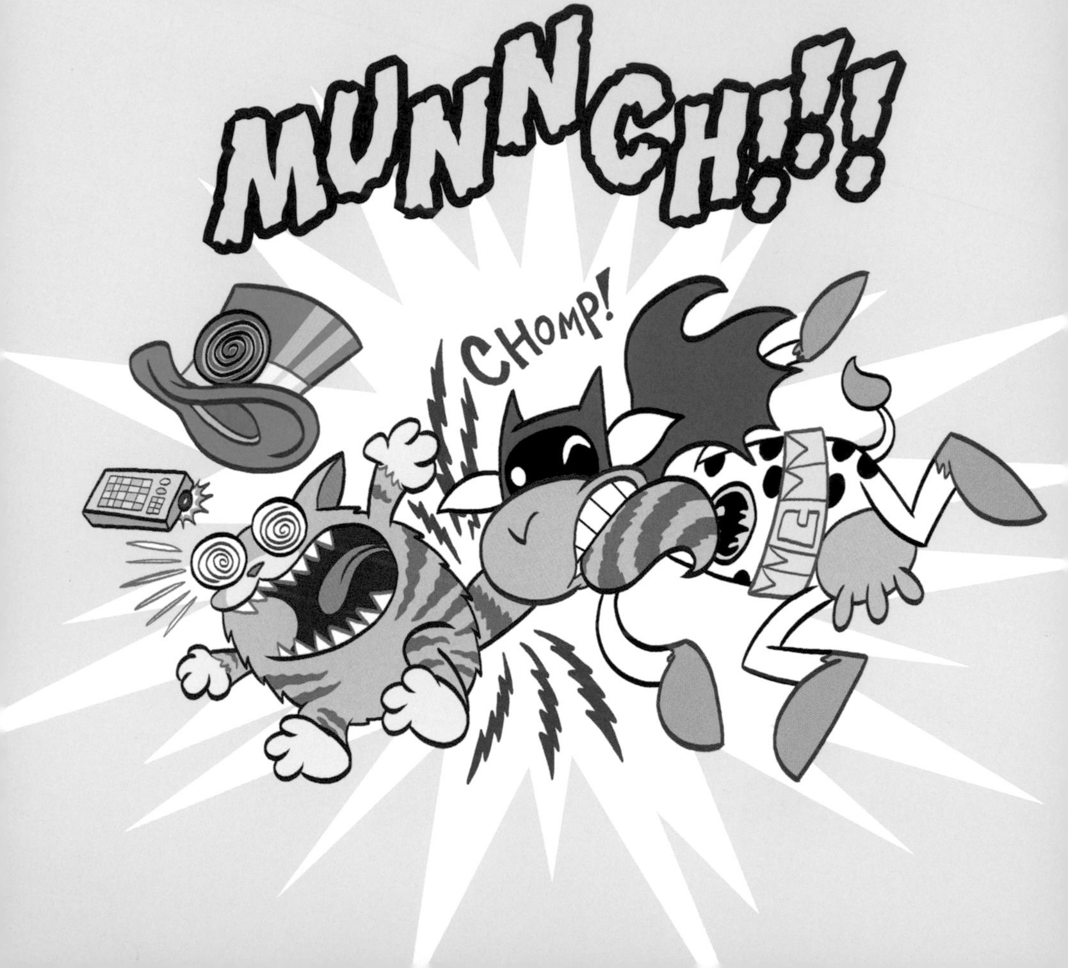
MUNNCH!!!
CHOMP!

"Mee-OW!" wailed the furry foe.

"Your adventure through the looking glass is over," Batcow said.

The hero lifted the Mad Catter up by the scruff of his neck. The top hat tumbled to the ground. Out popped a remote control. This was how the Catter controlled the devices in the party hats.

Batcow stomped on the gadget, causing it to short-circuit.

ZZRRRRT!!!

The barnyard animals were no longer brainwashed.

"How dare you!" hissed the Catter. He leaped at Batcow, but the hero held him at a distance. The furious feline clawed at nothing but air.

Batcow smiled. **"You'll be spending the rest of your nine lives behind bars,"** she said.

* * *

Soon after, the Gotham City Police arrived. They carted off the Mad Catter and the Crazy Kittens to prison. The city had just added a wing especially for criminal critters, and it was being put to good use!

Batcow helped the rest of the officers return all the stolen crops to their rightful owners.

Back at Merkel Meadows, none of the livestock remembered the wild tea party. They looked at the scattered party hats and shook their heads. The horses galloped slowly to their stables. The pigs pattered to their pens.

A few animals stayed behind to hang out with the day's hoofed hero, the Batcow.

"That must've been some party," said the little goat. "Too *baaad* we can't remember any of it."

"Indeed," the goat's father said. "But *Baaat*cow certainly has a tale to tell."

The chicken turned to the hero. "What was it like?" she clucked.

"Yeah," said the little goat. "Tell us the whole story from the beginning!"

"Please! Please!" chirped the chorus of little chicks.

Batcow looked sleepily 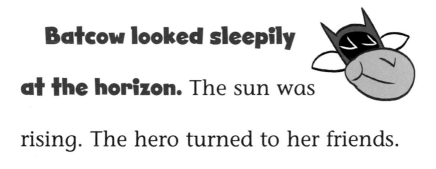 **at the horizon.** The sun was rising. The hero turned to her friends. She started acting out the story.

"All right," said the Super-Pet. "I'll

tell you everything I know. How did

it start? Oh, yes . . . Well, you see, Joe

MacDonald had a farm . . ." **END!**

KNOW YOUR HERO PETS!

1. Krypto
2. Streaky
3. Beppo
4. Comet
5. Super-Turtle
6. Fuzzy
7. Ace
8. Robin Robin
9. Batcow
10. Jumpa
11. Whatzit
12. Hoppy
13. Storm
14. Topo
15. Ark
16. Fluffy
17. Proty
18. Gleek
19. Big Ted
20. Dawg
21. Paw Pooch
22. Bull Dog
23. Chameleon Collie
24. Hot Dog
25. Tail Terrier
26. Tusky Husky
27. Mammoth Mutt
28. Rex the Wonder Dog
29. B'dg
30. Sen-Tag
31. Fendor
32. Stripezoid
33. Zallion
34. Ribitz
35. Bzzd
36. Gratch
37. Buzzoo
38. Fossfur
39. Zhoomp
40. Eeny

KNOW YOUR VILLAIN PETS!

1. Bizarro Krypto
2. Ignatius
3. Brainicat
4. Mechanikat
5. Crackers
6. Giggles
7. Joker Fish
8. Rozz
9. Artie Puffin
10. Griff
11. Waddles
12. Mad Catter
13. Dogwood
14. Chauncey
15. Misty
16. Sneezers
17. General Manx
18. Nizz
19. Fer-El
20. Titano
21. Mr. Mind
22. Sobek
23. Bit-Bit
24. X-43
25. Starro
26. Dex-Starr
27. Glomulus
28. Rhinoldo
29. Whoosh
30. Pronto
31. Snorrt
32. Rolf
33. Squealer
34. Kajunn
35. Tootz
36. Eezix
37. Donald
38. Waxxee
39. Fimble
40. Webbik

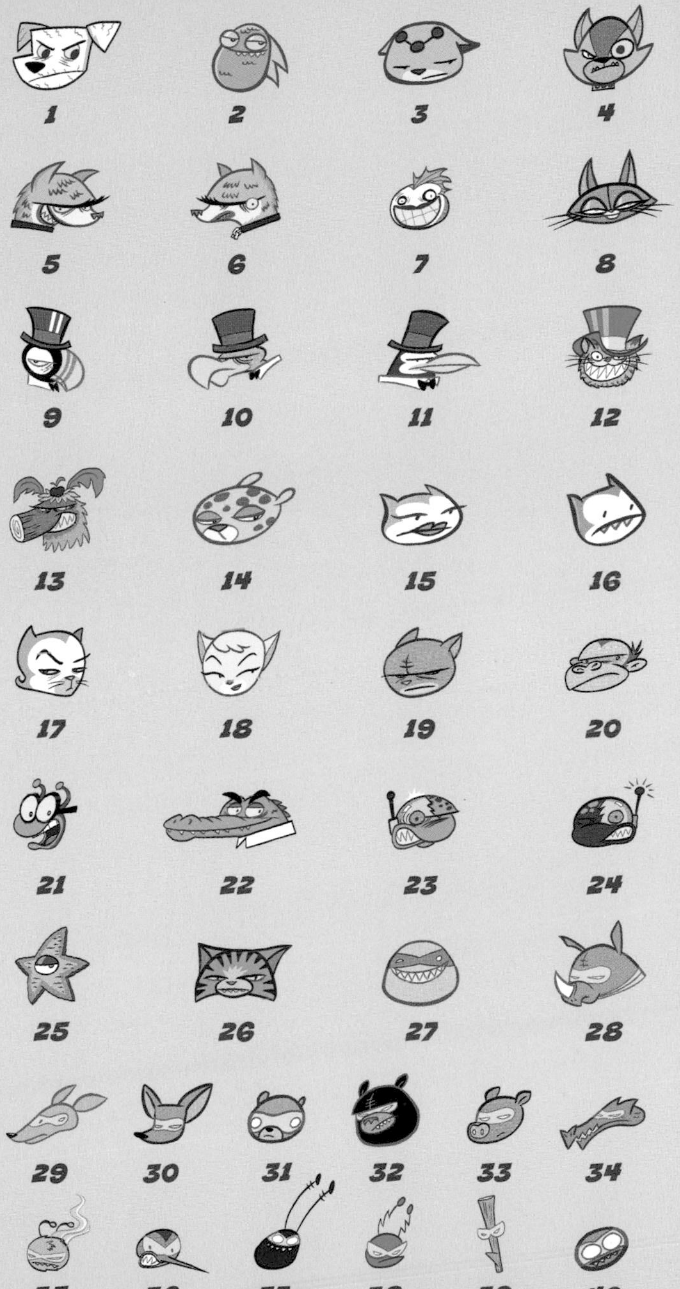
1 2 3 4
5 6 7 8
9 10 11 12
13 14 15 16
17 18 19 20
21 22 23 24
25 26 27 28
29 30 31 32 33 34
35 36 37 38 39 40

MEET THE AUTHOR!

John Sazaklis

John is super lucky to have written, and sometimes illustrated, many children's books about his favorite characters. To him, it's a dream come true. He has been reading comics and watching cartoons since before even the internet! John lives with his beautiful wife, Nicoletta, in the Big Apple.

MEET THE ILLUSTRATOR!

Eisner Award-winner Art Baltazar

Art Baltazar is a cartoonist machine from the heart of Chicago! He defines cartoons and comics not only as an art style, but as a way of life. Currently, Art is the creative force behind *The New York Times* best-selling, Eisner Award-winning, DC Comics series Tiny Titans, and the co-writer for *Billy Batson and the Magic of SHAZAM!* Art is living the dream! He draws comics and never has to leave the house. He lives with his lovely wife, Rose, big boy Sonny, little boy Gordon, and little girl Audrey. Right on!

WORD POWER!

brainwash (BRAYN-wahsh)—make someone accept and believe something

capers (KAY-purz)—criminal acts, or tricks or pranks

feline (FEE-line)—to do with cats, or like a cat

felon (FEL-uhn) —someone who has commited a serious crime

hypnotized (HIP-nuh-tized)—put someone into a trance

investigate (in-VESS-tuh-gate)—if you investigate something, such as a crime, you find out as much as possible about the crime in order to solve it

scheme (SKEEM)—a plan or plot for doing something, or to plan and plot something

startled (START-uhld)—surprised or frightened someone

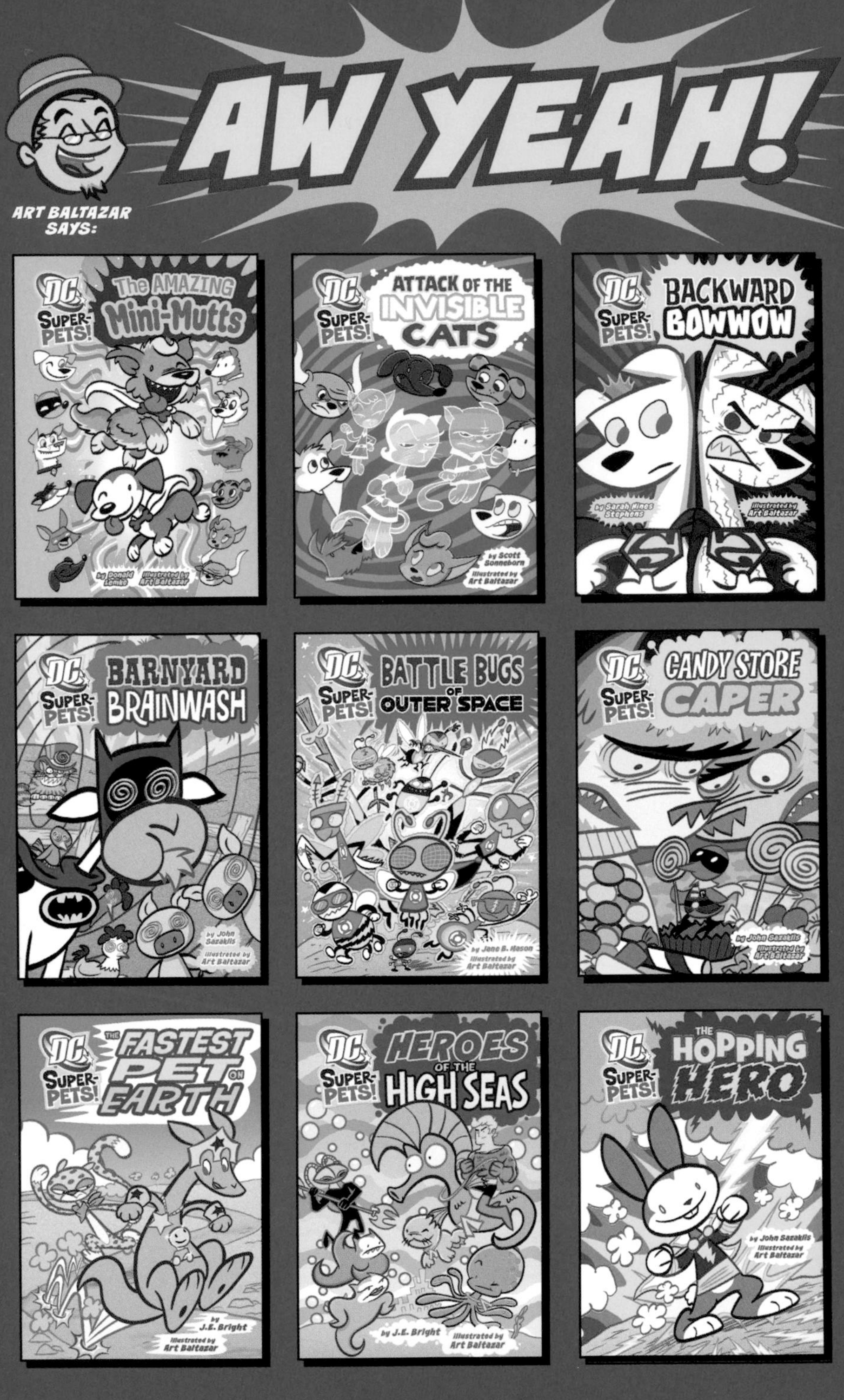
ART BALTAZAR SAYS:
AW YEAH!
DC SUPER-PETS! The AMAZING Mini-Mutts
by Donald Lemke
Illustrated by Art Baltazar
DC SUPER-PETS! ATTACK OF THE INVISIBLE CATS
by Scott Sonneborn
Illustrated by Art Baltazar
DC SUPER-PETS! BACKWARD BOWWOW
by Sarah Hines Stephens
Illustrated by Art Baltazar
DC SUPER-PETS! BARNYARD BRAINWASH
by John Sazaklis
Illustrated by Art Baltazar
DC SUPER-PETS! BATTLE BUGS OF OUTER SPACE
by Jane B. Mason
Illustrated by Art Baltazar
DC SUPER-PETS! CANDY STORE CAPER
by John Sazaklis
Illustrated by Art Baltazar
DC SUPER-PETS! THE FASTEST PET ON EARTH
by J.E. Bright
Illustrated by Art Baltazar
DC SUPER-PETS! HEROES OF THE HIGH SEAS
by J.E. Bright
Illustrated by Art Baltazar
DC SUPER-PETS! THE HOPPING HERO
by John Sazaklis
Illustrated by Art Baltazar

Read all of these totally awesome DC SUPER-PETS stories today!

THE FUN DOESN'T STOP HERE!

Discover more:

- **Videos & Contests!**
- **Games & Puzzles!**
- **Heroes & Villains!**
- **Authors & Illustrators!**

@ www.capstonekids.com

Find cool websites and more books like this one at www.facthound.com Just type in Book I.D. 9781404864832 and you're ready to go!

⊞ Picture Window Books™

Published in 2012
A Capstone Imprint
1710 Roe Crest Drive
North Mankato, MN 56003
www.capstonepub.com

STAR25286

Cataloging-in-Publication Data is available
at the Library of Congress website.
ISBN: 978-1-4048-6483-2 (library binding)
ISBN: 978-1-4048-7213-4 (paperback)

Summary: On a farm outside Gotham City,
the cows have gone mad, and the roosters
are cock-a-doodle cuckoo. Only one crazy
kitten could have brainwashed this barnyard
. . . the evil Mad Catter. If the Batcow can't
stop the loony goon, this farm frenzy will
quickly become udder madness!

Art Director & Designer: Bob Lentz
Editor: Donald Lemke
Creative Director: Heather Kindseth
Editorial Director: Michael Dahl

Printed in the United States of America
in Stevens Point, Wisconsin.
072012   006878R

DC™

SUPER-PETS!

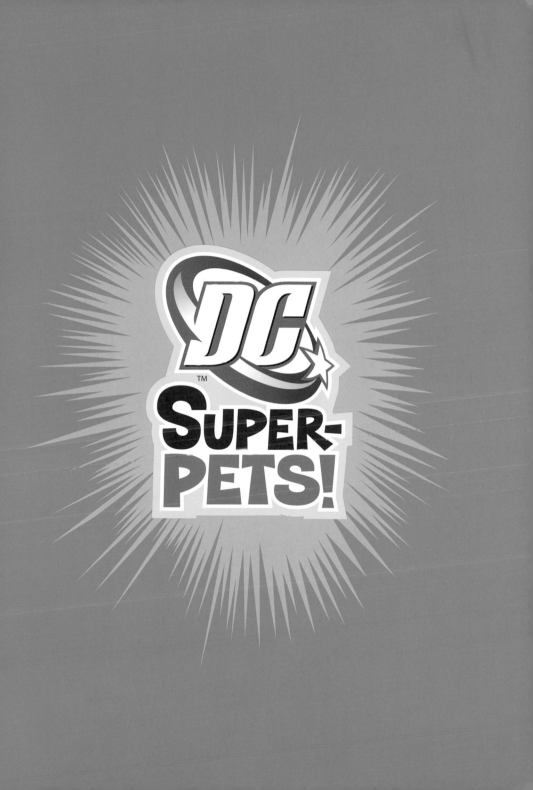

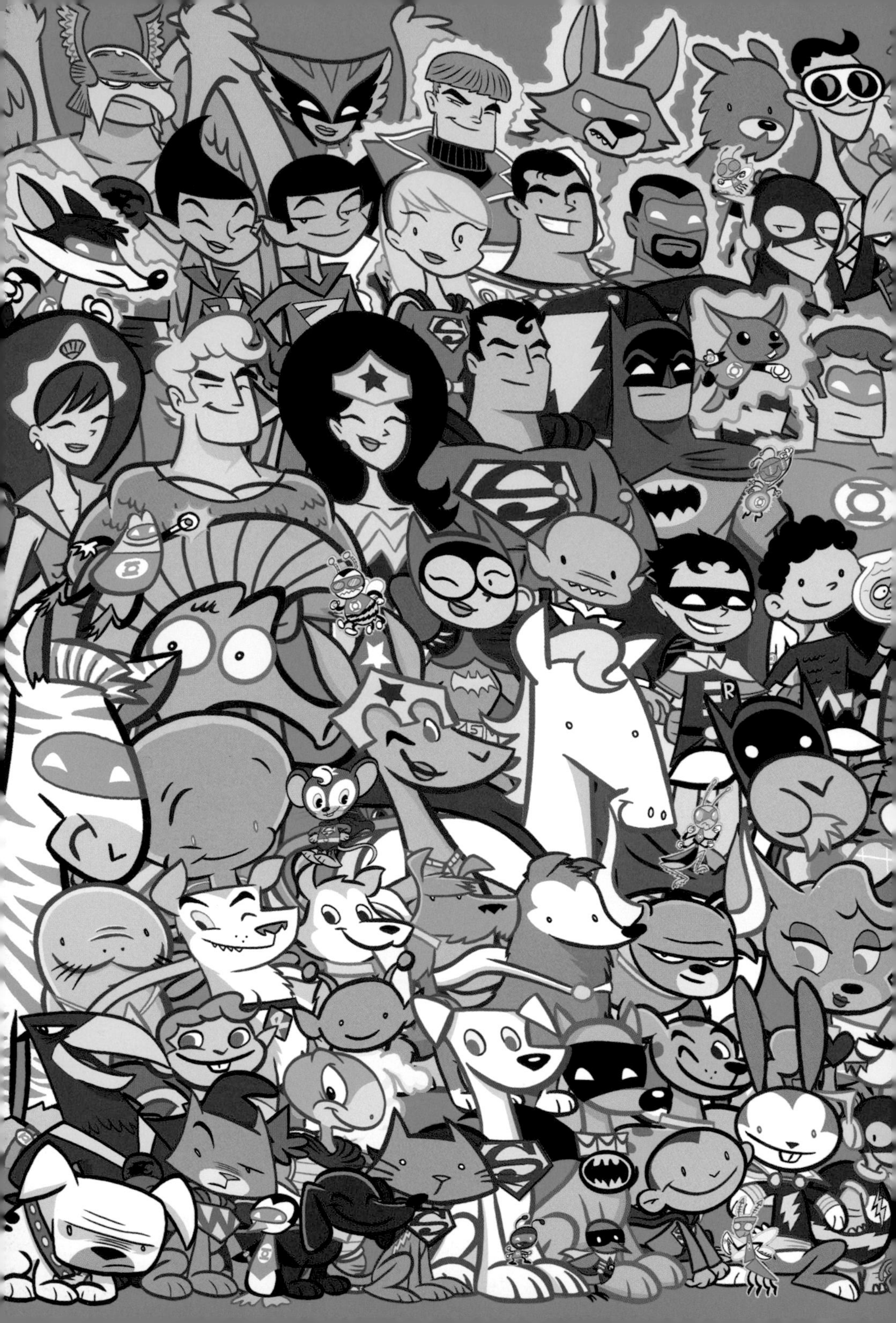

DC™

SUPER-PETS!

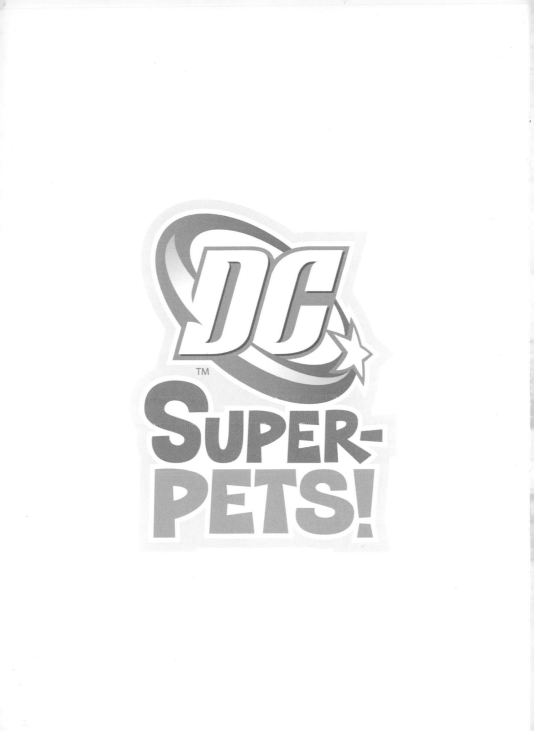

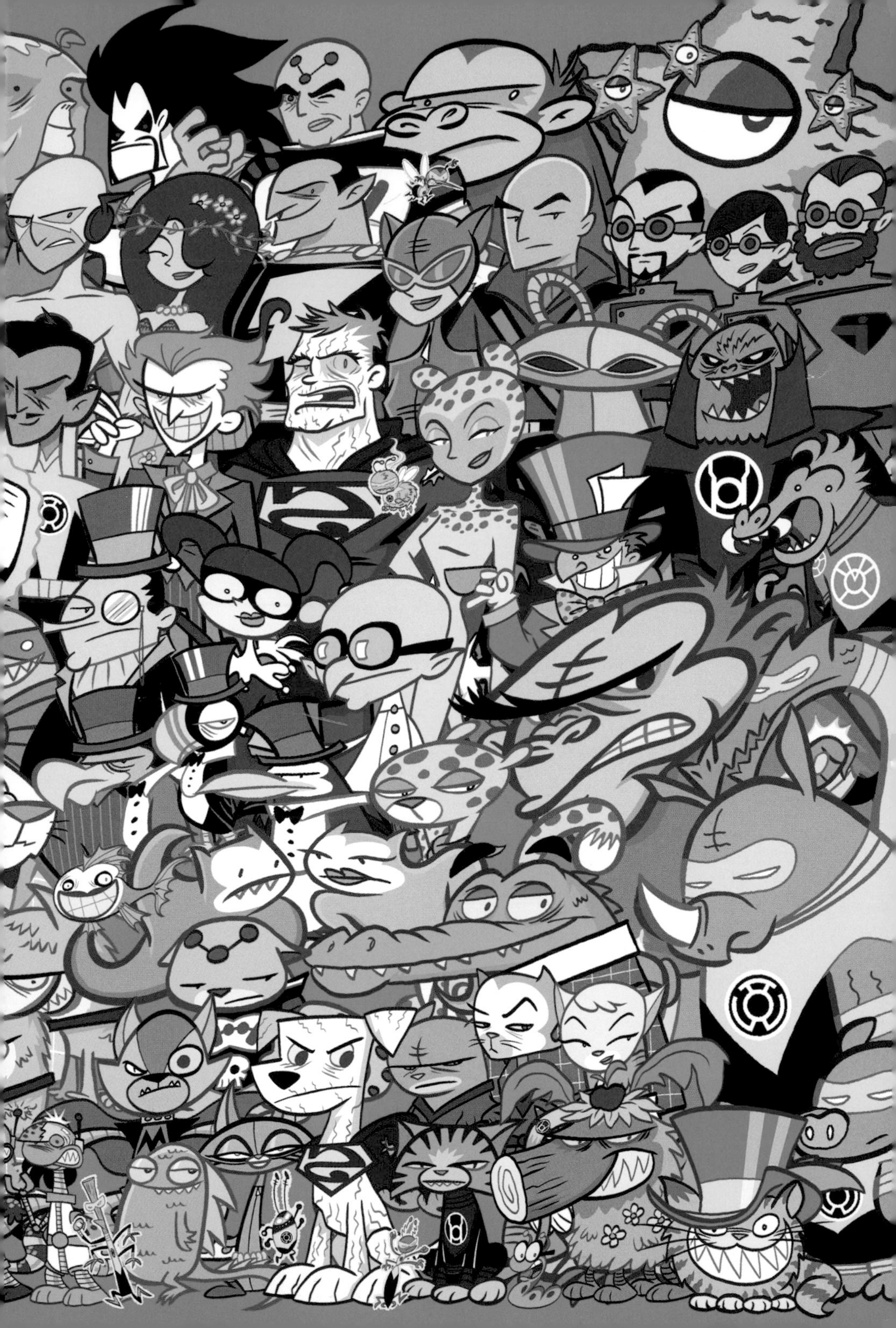